Once U

Holiday Tales of *Pride & Prejudice*

Rose Fairbanks

Once Upon a December

Published by Rose Fairbanks

Several passages in this novel are paraphrased from the works of Jane Austen.

Table of Contents

A Sleigh Ride for Two	5
Thawed Hearts	31
Fitzy the Snowman	39
The Force of Love	49
Home with You	77
Fortune Favours the Bold	83
Winter Walks	93
Darcy's Christmas Wish by Penelope Swan	97
Also by Rose Fairbanks	111
Acknowledgments	112
About the Author	113

A Sleigh Ride for Two

Fitzwilliam Darcy and his guest and best friend, Charles Bingley, looked to the clock on the mantle in the dining room of Darcy House. Agreeing it was time to re-join the ladies, and after rousing Bingley's brother-in-law, they returned to the drawing room and greeted their sisters.

"Ladies!" Bingley declared. "I have the most exciting news. Darcy has found an estate for sale, which should meet my needs. It is only thirty miles from Pemberley!"

In a rare moment of shared emotion, both gentlemen observed the calm smiles and restrained happiness of the ladies and were reminded of a family of women with much more irrepressible feelings. Their thoughts on the Bennet family differed entirely, though. Bingley never minded the exuberance of Mrs. Bennet and the younger daughters; the angelic, if cryptic, smile of Jane Bennet could make him tolerate anything. Darcy could only repine the absence of Elizabeth Bennet.

"I hope you are not planning to move there now, Charles," said the eldest of the Bingley siblings.

"Whyever not, Louisa?" the younger sister, Caroline, asked.

"Think of how cold it must be in winter!"

Darcy hid a smile at Caroline's concerned look. "I was told in the last letter from my steward that there is already a heavy blanket of snow."

"But surely that is of little consequence to us. We would winter in London, as always."

Bingley deferred to his friend's knowledge. "I usually spend the worst months at Pemberley, actually," Darcy said. "Roads need repair, and tenant houses must be secured against the cold and snow, among other matters." Not that he would mention the increased demand on his mines during the winter. Caroline did not need to know that he had even more than ten thousand pounds per annum.

"Yet you remain here now," she purred with a knowing look.

Darcy bristled. He would prefer not to think about why he was not wintering at Pemberley, ridiculous fool that he was. "Your brother's estate is thirty miles to the north of

Pemberley." He hoped that knowledge would make her less enamoured with things North.

"Fitzwilliam is remaining in London because I wish it," Georgiana intervened. She did not care for Caroline's criticism of her brother, and even worse, he was unknowingly encouraging her again. She knew he thought he was persuading her that Pemberley was unlikeable, but what Caroline likely heard was him giving her every reason to stay in London—where he was.

Her brother was very intelligent but a ridiculous dunderhead when it came to ladies. She sighed; sometimes she truly feared Pemberley would fall to her line. Of course, that would mean her brother would allow her to grow up and marry. No matter how well deserved his anger was over her ill-advised attempt at an elopement this past summer, she was rather certain he meant to keep her a child always.

Surprisingly, it was Louisa who turned the conversation back to its origin. "I imagine you are quite homebound in the winter. What carriage can go through all that snow?"

"Oh! We have sleighs!" Georgiana replied and belatedly realised she was far too enthusiastic. Not only was it unladylike—and clearly astonished her brother—but the setting could be quite romantic. The last thing Fitzwilliam needed was Caroline attempting to get him alone in a sleigh with her. She shuddered at the thought and almost burst out in laughter as she saw her brother do the same. Then his face took on a softened look that intrigued her immensely. She glanced to Mr. Bingley, who shared the expression.

"Darcy, is there anyone in London who sells sleighs?"

"Of course..." He would have said more but was interrupted by Caroline.

"I am certain they are vastly superior here than in the country towns."

"I could acquaint you with my favourite shop tomorrow," Darcy continued, ignoring Caroline.

"Excellent."

"Do you know any more about the estate, Mr. Darcy?" Caroline attempted again to garner his attention. She had beauty, wealth, accomplishments, and her brother was his best friend. She only needed patience and persistence. She had every confidence she would win her gentleman.

Georgiana tapped her shoe against Darcy's, their arranged cue that she would deal with Caroline. "Georgiana actually would know more about the kinds of things that would interest ladies."

Looking at Hurst, Darcy arose to refresh the glasses of his male guests and made his escape. Georgiana managed to keep Caroline's attention for a few minutes and then invited her to perform on the pianoforte. Soon Hurst was falling asleep, and Caroline and Louisa fawned over Georgiana's performance. Darcy and Bingley discussed their plans for meeting on the morrow. They would meet at the shop and return to Darcy House together. Their respective sisters had need of the carriages, but they could hire one.

Leaving Darcy House, Caroline was more confident than ever that she may soon become Mrs. Darcy. Louisa was determined to become better acquainted with her in-laws, who lived in a mild climate, while her husband prayed Darcy would never run out of his good port. Their brother was forming a desperate resolution. Georgiana went to her chambers dissatisfied with the evening. Her brother was in a testy mood and had been for weeks. She allowed him to ruminate alone in the library, where he wondered if he would ever cease to long for a pair of fine eyes.

*****

The next day, Darcy and Bingley met at the appointed time and place. After reviewing all the equipment, Bingley settled on a stylish sleigh made for two.

"Why the rush to purchase one this winter? For all our talk last night, you are unlikely to take possession before March."

Bingley quickly paid the clerk and made arrangements for it to be delivered to Hurst's townhouse instead of answering Darcy.

"I am certain Mr. Latimer would allow you to store the sleigh at the estate."

"It is not meant for Lethenbrook Bridge. I am going to have it transported to Netherfield."

Bingley attempted to rush from the establishment, but Darcy threw out an arm, blocking his path.

"What do you mean?"

Bingley was surprised by the anger in Darcy's voice. He pushed past him, and the men hired a carriage to resume their conversation.

"I am to own an estate! And I can still think of only one woman I wish to make its mistress. I will now be hundreds of miles from her family! That must surely remove some of your complaints."

Darcy groaned in disgust. He agreed distance from the Bennets would remove many of his objections. Hence he stayed in London, where he could not quite long for Elizabeth to be present in his country home.

"It does not remove the issue of Miss Bennet's attachment to you."

"I believe I am glad you perceived no admiration. She is not like the women you are used to being around. For you to see her sentiments, you must be the recipient of them."

"Clearly you see only what you wish to see."

"I never disagreed with you on the other ladies."

"You are merely more bewitched by Miss Bennet."

"By your report, she has nothing to bewitch with."

"She is pretty."

"Pretty! She is the most beautiful woman I have ever seen and has been since first sight! You even acknowledged her as the only handsome lady in attendance at the first ball we attended."

"Impossible!" Darcy quickly declared. He recalled liking Elizabeth too much, wishing to find fault in her, but surely he always found her lovely.

"Well, if you refuse to believe you found her handsome at the time—despite your words that I perfectly recall—then, what is bewitching me? Perhaps I find her so beautiful because I love her."

Darcy did not reply at first. He entirely agreed with the sentiment. Elizabeth was perfection, but he was aware that he found her more beautiful as his regard deepened. Never mind, it did not negate the concern for Miss Bennet's attachment.

"You have still only proven you are blinded. I am impartial and find her indifferent. At best she would marry you to secure her family, and at worst refuse you."

"If she did not like me, then why did she not discourage me?"

"She would not wish to wound your heart."

"But she would think marrying me with indifference or rejecting me would not hurt my feelings?"

Finally stumped, Darcy grew silent. At last he could only say, "She is simply too reserved. Look at her family! She is the only one who does not make it clear what she feels on any matter."

Bingley laughed at such an image. "Oh yes, now you mock discretion! And reserve? As if you should speak! You cannot talk me out of this. I am returning to Netherfield and will return with a bride."

Darcy sat in sullen silence until just before they arrived at his door. "You will declare yourself immediately?"

"I had planned to propose on a sleigh ride."

"She would ride with you unaccompanied?"

"You think not?"

"I am certain Mrs. Bennet would allow it, but I do not think your Miss Bennet would agree."

Bingley deflated. It was the perfect image he had in his head. "What if there is a chaperone? Miss Elizabeth...I could buy another sleigh, and she could ride with someone. That is not so bad."

Darcy's eyes widened as he imagined just who Elizabeth could ride in a sleigh with. Wickham was likely a favourite at their house by now. Would she nestle in close with him? Would he see her cheeks turn rosy with the cold and offer to hold her close, providing heat? Would he make her laugh? And when she turned to face him, with that irresistible twinkle in her eyes, would he lean in and touch those tempting lips with his vile ones?

His throat was tight, but he must speak. “I will come.”

Bingley raised an eyebrow, a suspicion beginning to form, but he said nothing.

Darcy only added, “Do not inform your sister of your intentions or that I am coming as well.”

He exited the carriage and went directly to his library, penning a note that he wished to buy the same sleigh as his friend, both to be delivered to Netherfield Park, Hertfordshire.

*****

“He has come!” Mrs. Bennet burst into Jane and Elizabeth’s room a day or two later. “John said he saw Mr. Bingley and Mr. Darcy coming up the lane. Make haste!”

Jane had yet to begin her toilette, but Elizabeth was finished and promptly sent downstairs.

She expected Mr. Bingley to be as amiable as ever but was surprised when Mr. Darcy stood so hastily he almost tripped over his own feet. “Miss Elizabeth,” he said with a bow.

Mr. Bingley stifled his laughter at his friend's expense and performed his piece of civility. Soon they were all seated as they heard the muffled sounds of five other women readying for the day.

"What a pleasant surprise this is! We were assured you meant to return to Netherfield no more this winter," Elizabeth put forward. She hoped for confirmation that his sisters had been behind the deceit. She had imagined his friend was as well, and yet Mr. Darcy was present now.

"I am sorry to make you think that. I was delayed. Darcy was helping me find an estate to purchase." Bingley wanted to beat his chest in pride.

Elizabeth furrowed her brow. Was he not remaining at Netherfield? "And how long will you be at Netherfield then?"

"Darcy must return next week, but I am uncertain how long I will remain. Quite possibly until I take possession of Lethenbrook Bridge."

She heaved a relieved sigh and replied cheerfully, "How nice it will be to have you here for Christmas then! Sir William Lucas always hosts a great party just a few days before. Jane particularly enjoys this time of year."

"Does she?" Bingley felt lightheaded with anticipation.

After what felt like an eternity, Jane came down, and Elizabeth believed she looked lovelier than ever. She smiled widely at Mr. Bingley. Mrs. Bennet stayed only for a moment before claiming to need to speak with the housekeeper. It was clear to all that she hoped to come up with some excuse to get rid of Elizabeth and Darcy.

For her part, Jane could scarcely help blushing or even meet Mr. Bingley's eye. But every time he spoke, she replied, praying he would continue the conversation. Hearing his voice, if she could not meet his eye, was soothing.

Miss Bennet's obvious enjoyment of Bingley's presence struck Darcy. He studied her closely and saw that his friend was correct. She was not like Elizabeth, so obvious in her enjoyment of things, but he could see her preference now.

Elizabeth entirely ignored his presence. He had not thought about it until now; he was always satisfied with observing her when she gave others her attention. Now he began to wonder if she disliked him, a thought that naturally led to a quick surmise of whom she did like. It might not be a romantic interlude, but he was more determined than ever to get her in the sleigh with him. He would clear his name.

Bingley could contain himself no more and blurted out, “Darcy and I brought a pair of sleighs with us today. We thought you ladies might enjoy a ride.”

“Oh! A sleigh ride!” Jane cried before sobering. “Elizabeth and I do not know how to drive…”

Bingley laughed, and even Darcy smiled. “We had hoped there would be no harm in being your escorts,” Bingley clarified.

Jane looked to Elizabeth and silently beseeched her to agree.

“I will just go and ask Mama,” Elizabeth said.

Darcy had been watching Elizabeth intently and saw that she was not entirely at ease with the scheme. After Elizabeth exited, he excused himself under the guise of checking on the horses. He hoped to speak somehow with Elizabeth about her apprehension. Instead, he overheard the conversation with her mother

“There is nothing to be done for. Jane would not go on her own; you will have to bear Mr. Darcy, as dreadful as he is.”

“Mama, he will hear you! Besides, I would not wish for Jane to go on her own either.”

“You will never get a husband! When I think of how you turned Mr. Collins down—

turned all of this down! Well, perhaps I do wish Mr. Darcy on you then. Only do not allow him to vex you as he normally does. Mr. Wickham may call later, and I do not wish you to be out of spirits."

Elizabeth rolled her eyes and sighed as her mother marched away. She began walking to the door, swallowing her fears, when Mr. Darcy unexpectedly came from a doorway.

Already too nervous, she jumped. "Mr. Darcy! How—how long have you been in the hallway?"

He raised an eyebrow at her, and she could not explain why the sound of his hushed voice sent a chill down her body.

"Quite long enough. I must speak with you."

She swallowed. "Certainly. I believe it is only balls that make me silent and taciturn."

He chuckled, the sound rumbling from his chest. Noticing his chest caused Elizabeth to realise how broad he was; could they even fit in a sleigh together?

"I believe I might say some things that will anger you, but I know my friend would like a very peaceful, quiet, and long ride with your sister."

"Does he have something of importance to say to her?"

"Yes."

As he spoke, she had retrieved her coat from a cupboard, and he gallantly helped her, causing her to blush.

"If you are ready, madam." Darcy extended his arm, and Elizabeth gravely took it.

Taking in her expression, Darcy hoped to tease. "I do not bite."

She managed a small smile. "No, but they do." She nodded at the horses.

He stopped walking and looked at her in surprise. "The horses frighten you?"

"Ever since I was a child. I even dislike carriage rides; they seem so unruly at times."

"Elizabeth Bennet admits to fear!"

"I admit to facing my fears. I am going on the ride."

Darcy could hardly help the bit of pride he felt when he added to himself, *with me, Sweetheart*.

He handed her in and helped arrange the warm bricks around her feet. Then he held out the large blanket for her to wrap snugly around her lap. They waited for Jane and Bingley to situate themselves.

At last Darcy urged the horses forward, and Elizabeth was not the least bit ashamed when she momentarily clutched his arm.

"Do you do this often?" she asked.

"It is the only way to drive in the winter near my estate. My sister and I spend many hours out of doors like this."

She smiled brightly. "Just sleigh rides?"

He replied cryptically. "There are many things to do out of doors in the winter."

"Mr. Darcy of Pemberley skates and throws snowballs? I am uncertain I can believe it."

"Why should it be so impossible?"

"I had not thought you were given to merriment, sir."

"When in the right company, I can be."

"Oh, of course." And Hertfordshire was not the right company.

"You misunderstand me."

"Do I? I have heard you can be very agreeable amongst those you count as friends."

Darcy frowned before speaking. "I am certain Mr. Wickham has said all manner of things about me."

"It was Miss Bingley, in fact, who told Jane that even as you offended all of Meryton your first night at the ball!"

"I did not have any acquaintance outside of my party."

"And no one can be introduced in a ballroom?"

"You are correct; I should have judged better. I would have wished to be introduced to you that night."

Elizabeth could not resist her reply though it was not as saucy as she had intended. "I believe you had such an opportunity."

A chill ran down Darcy's spine. He had soon regretted those words he said at the assembly, not merely because he found Elizabeth quite pretty but because he was raised to behave well, and he knew he had not. And now he knew Elizabeth's first impression of him was of such ungentlemanly conduct!

"I should have danced with you, Elizabeth."

She blushed but for some reason could not bear to correct him.

"Why did you not then?" Her heart was beating quickly, and she hated herself for it. She held her breath.

"I was in a foul mood, and quite frankly, you caught me behaving dreadfully."

She despised the sinking feeling she had. Of course, he should have only danced with her out of civility. She could not remain silent and seem affected, however. "I suppose you attempted to rectify your mistake at Lucas Lodge then."

He smiled a little. "No, at Lucas Lodge I desired to dance with the lady whose fine eyes I had been admiring for a fortnight."

Confused, she scolded, "Could you not see Jane's preference for Mr. Bingley? And his for her? Well, no wonder you were in such a foul mood! In love with the lady your best friend admires."

"Good God, no!" Darcy was so shocked by her misunderstanding that his words escaped without thought. "No, I did not see her preference, nor his."

Colour rose in Elizabeth's cheeks. "You did mean to separate them! I can hardly suppose what made you give her up, and no matter how awful you have acted all these weeks keeping him away, I thank you for returning him."

Again speaking without thought, Darcy explained, "I attempted to separate them because your family is of no consequence and is intolerable, not because I fancy your sister."

"Oh, so even the handsomest woman in Hertfordshire is not enough to tempt you! Thank you for explaining so clearly how dreadful a connection with my family must be. Do not worry, sir, we would hardly want to be connected with you either."

They rode in silence for a moment, but he could have sworn Elizabeth was shivering.

"Are you warm enough?"

"I am perfectly tolerable."

He closed his eyes in guilt. "I am sorry. It is natural to have these concerns about marriage."

"Why should you be the judge of your friend's happiness?"

"Because I was judging my own as well!"

"What?"

"You! I wanted to dance with you! I want to…God help me, you are the most exasperating woman I have ever met in my life, but I want to marry you!"

"Oh yes, merely tolerable can tempt you to matrimony." He was insufferable.

"This is the answer I am to expect?"

"How did you think I would answer when you tell me you like me against your will and character, insult my family and situation in life, and admit to trying to destroy my sister's happiness?"

"So, if I had flattered you, I would have been accepted?"

"Been accepted? Did you believe you asked a question? But despite all this, your character was made plain to me by Mr. Wickham."

"You take too eager an interest in his concerns."

"Who can help but to take an interest in his concerns when they know of his troubles placed on him by you?"

"Troubles? Oh yes, they have been great indeed!"

He was so enraged, he did not focus on his driving. The horses stumbled on an embankment. Elizabeth cried out and careened into Darcy's side. He quickly caught her to him as he righted the horses. Elizabeth trembled in her fear.

"Release me," she hissed when he did not. "In fact, we should call out to Jane and Mr. Bingley as we have been gone quite a while."

"Are you too cold?"

"No."

He brushed his nose, the only exposed part of him, against her cheek, and she gasped.

"You are like ice! You are correct; we must turn around."

He was about to call out to Bingley when she disagreed. "No, please. I can bear it. Jane is more delicate than I, and she has not asked to turn. She has waited so long to see him again, and if his errand is as you say, then I would give them all the time in the world."

"Then you will allow me to keep you warm."

"I am not your sister to take care of, Mr. Darcy."

"No, not my sister at all. I apologise. I meant to discuss this when we first set out, but I am always so lost when in your presence."

Elizabeth blushed a little and was amazed to discover he believed himself in her power.

"Mr. Wickham is the son of my father's steward..." Darcy continued to tell Elizabeth of his past with Wickham. She was surprised to hear the truth about the living and astonished and disgusted to hear of his deception of Georgiana.

"How blind I have been!" she cried to herself. "How prejudiced and partial!"

"It was my prejudice, first. If I had not behaved so poorly in the country, then you would have questioned his story. But there has been no harm. You are safe."

She shook her head. "No harm? I have abused you horribly throughout the Meryton area."

"It is no less than I deserve."

"No! You are an honourable man, how can you say it of yourself? How can you make me blameless?"

He took her hand and squeezed it, and she knew. He had not directly said it before, but now he was declaring himself without words. He loved her. He could forgive her so easily because he loved her.

She allowed him to hold her hand as her stomach flipped at the revelation. She considered what a wonderland she was in, to be loved by Fitzwilliam Darcy!

More astonishing was the realisation that she could forgive him as well. He was not perfect, but neither was she. He had looked to find fault, but so had she. She imagined more than she ever saw. She had previously determined that vanity was the cause of her blindness, but now she thought better. As misdirected as it was, only one thing could cause that kind of blindness. Her throat was too tight to speak lest she break the fairy spell.

At last Bingley had turned the sleigh around, and if Darcy could think of anything other than Elizabeth nestled close to his side, he would have laughed at how long it must have taken his friend. A shiver passed through Elizabeth, and he looked at her in concern.

"You are too cold! Here, we will cover you with my blanket as well."

"No, I am well." She truly was.

Disbelieving her, Darcy leaned to check the coolness of her cheek with his nose again, but unexpectedly—although delightfully—Elizabeth tilted her face up just an inch, and his lips landed on hers. They pulled back in surprise, and Elizabeth immediately blushed scarlet. He pulled the team aside.

"If that is what it takes to warm your cheeks, then I am afraid I will have to repeat it," Darcy said huskily.

Elizabeth looked up at him through hooded eyes. "You did say you would not take care of me as you would your sister."

"Elizabeth," he said as she slid her arms around his waist. Nothing had felt more right in the world than when he felt Elizabeth's timid smile against his lips.

It was too cold for more than a few brief kisses, and they soon set out to catch up with Jane and Bingley. When they met up again at Longbourn, congratulations for their friends were quite in order.

Warming by the fire in the drawing room with fresh tea and coffee, Darcy approached

Elizabeth. "I believe that was singularly the best sleigh ride I have ever experienced."

Elizabeth smiled fondly. It certainly was one to remember all of her life. "Is it to be your last, sir?"

"No, I do not believe it will be."

"Then it is only the best you have experienced so far. Who knows how many more pleasant sleigh rides are in your future."

Darcy laughed. Dear God, he loved this woman.

Jane and Bingley saw it all across the room and admitted to their hopes.

*****

Two weeks later, Georgiana Darcy was unsurprised to be summoned to Netherfield, where her brother was unexpectedly staying, again, for several weeks. She had heard enough of Miss Bingley's extreme dislike of Elizabeth Bennet to understand the source of Darcy's foul mood from weeks before. She arrived on the very day of a party at Sir William Lucas's.

Elizabeth and Darcy's eyes were shining brightly, having made good use of their sleigh ride that morning. Gathering with their friends, and even the family Darcy had come to appreciate, was the perfect ending to their day. The next morning, Darcy would approach Mr. Bennet to ask formally for Elizabeth's hand in marriage.

When dancing broke out, the engaged couples took the floor, and Darcy even granted permission for Georgiana to stand up with Sir William's eldest son. That night the residents of Netherfield Park and Longbourn knew a happiness found only in the warmth of the love of family. When Bingley received a letter from his sisters confirming everyone in their house was suffering from a terrible cold, he could only shrug and wonder at it being the London air. He had hopes yet for his sisters to join him at his estate in the North the next winter and looked forward to a great many more sleigh rides. Here again, his friend was in perfect agreement.

The End

Thawed Hearts

"Were they cold, Fitzwilliam?"

Darcy's younger sister's usual question interrupted his memories. Their father began telling the story of Christmas as a question and answer session when Darcy was a child. It had become a tradition, Darcy continuing when his father died.

Jesus was not born in December, but such things were difficult to explain to children. Generations of Darcy children were quite aware of how cold winters could be as they always spent them at their estate in Derbyshire. All his life, Darcy had known coldness and, usually, bleakness in December. Last Christmas, Georgiana had asked to skip the story. Looking back, Darcy should have realised that was the moment she decided to cast aside her childhood. The decision culminated in what she perceived was a very grown up decision to elope with a man whom she thought she loved. To hear her request the story this year soothed Darcy's guilty heart. The holiday was always difficult for him as he had even grimmer memories than Georgiana.

He pulled her a little closer to his side as they—just the two of them, always just the two of them—sat in the expansive drawing room.

"It was a bleak midwinter. The frosty wind blew hard; the ponds were all frozen over, and there was so much snow. Snow on snow; snow on snow."

He understood now. His father had explained it this way as a metaphor for the condition of the world as a whole before the Saviour's birth.

"But Heaven could not hold God's love, and so he sent his Son, a king born in a humble manger."

"A king? Everyone at the palace must have been very happy." Georgiana repeated the words that he first said on impulse and then repeated with each passing year until, in time, he taught her.

He shook his head. "Angels and archangels—all the cherubims and seraphims of Heaven—gathered near, but only His mother bestowed a kiss."

He held back the tears threatening to escape as he recalled the many times his mother held a small baby in her arms. As if in perfect reflection of the Saviour being born just to die, his mother had to give her life for the one sibling who would survive.

"What can I give Him? I have nothing to offer a king."

They both smiled as they reached their favourite part of the story.

"If you were a shepherd, what would you bring?"

"A lamb."

"And if you were a wise man?"

"I would do my part."

"Those are precious gifts to give. Well, dearest girl, what can you give Him?"

"I can give my heart."

Darcy looked over as Georgiana quietly cried. Handing her his handkerchief, he kissed her temple.

"Next time when you give your heart away, the man will know how precious it is."

She laid her head on his shoulder, and he sighed. In time she recovered, and the siblings continued through the motions of a holiday that brought more grief than cheer.

Two weeks later, Darcy and his sister had arrived in London. Darcy was to call at a friend's and invite him to dinner the following evening. Of course, any invitation to Bingley had to include the rest of his family. Still, Mrs.

Annesley said it was good practice for Georgiana. Heaven knew few people in the ton were pleasant, so his sister may as well learn to entertain them.

The butler led him down the hall to the drawing room and was about to announce him when Miss Bingley loudly exclaimed, "What do you mean you see no concern in Jane Bennet being in Town? You heard her! She has come all this way to try and ensnare Charles!"

The butler cleared his throat. "Mr. Darcy to see Mr. Bingley."

Both ladies straightened and Caroline spoke. "Oh yes, do be seated, Mr. Darcy. Charles, I regret, is out at the moment."

Darcy kept his call brief, but when the ladies separated at the subsequent dinner, he examined his friend's morose demeanour.

"You do not look well," he said, startling Bingley.

"I am well...only...forlorn, I suppose."

"Because of your disappointment?"

"Yes."

"I am certain my opinion means little, but I am unsure it is a great loss. She was handsome but spoke so little and smiled too much."

"Yes, and I know your views on their connections and lack of wealth."

"You are incorrect. I only cautioned you on those subjects. If she gave you her heart, and you gave her yours, it would be quite sufficient."

Perhaps it was the effects of the season on him—undoubtedly he was more melancholy this year than usual—but Darcy had a moment of clarity.

"Bingley...I must tell you...I overheard your sisters speaking yesterday. Miss Bennet is in Town. I believe she even called on them."

Bingley's eyes widened. "And what are you thinking?"

"I think that is not the action of an indifferent lady."

"Do you think she could love me?"

Darcy paused for a long moment and considered all he knew of Jane Bennet. To declare his opinions again would be selfish when Bingley felt such attachment. He could at least offer the gift of hope. "I still wonder how easily her heart can be touched, but if she truly cares for you and not your wealth, then you have gained a very great gift indeed."

"Thank you for telling me, my friend. I will endeavour to earn her heart; I know I already gave her mine."

Darcy managed a small smile. Although the wind howled outside, and they faced months of a bleak London winter, a warm ember of hope emerged. Perhaps Christmastide need not be a time for mourning and solitude but for Goodwill towards his loved ones and fellow creatures. He did not wish to gain a reputation as having the propensity to hate everyone. His smile grew as he considered those words and many others—along with the looks and charm—of Elizabeth Bennet.

A little over ten weeks later, Darcy read a much blotted note from his friend as he prepared to leave to visit his aunt's estate in Kent. He was able to recognise the words "marriage," "angel," and "Longbourn." He truly was happy to learn of Bingley's engagement. Bingley's courtship with Miss Bennet had proven to Darcy—who frequently accompanied his friend to Jane's aunt and uncle's house—they were well-matched and their sentiments equal.

More than realising his friend's affections were returned, he realised how officious and selfish his interference would have been. As he began to give more with his heart rather than be ruled by his fearful mind, the winter in his life thawed. Even Georgiana noticed, and her spirits improved.

Darcy considered how much he wished to join his friend's ranks of marrying with only the gift of hearts. He would begin again—with the one who held his heart—at his friend's wedding. He knew not when that would be but resolved to be patient and hope.

A week later, he laughed outright when his aunt announced a Miss Elizabeth Bennet, the particular friend of her rector's wife, stayed at the parsonage a mile from her house. Spring had arrived in Kent, and now in Fitzwilliam Darcy's heart as well. The winters to come in Derbyshire would always prove cold and snowy but no longer bleak.

The End

*Based on the poem *In the Bleak Midwinter* by Christina Rossetti

Fitzy the Snowman

Mama had let my siblings and me sit in the drawing room at my aunt and uncle Bennet's house to meet the visitors. We were to remain behind at our house in London, but our cousin, Jane, had recently become engaged. The wedding would be after Twelfth Night, so Mama and Papa arranged to stay a little longer than they usually did on their annual trip to Longbourn and brought us children with them. The carriage ride was cold and tiresome, but the morning after we arrived, we were greeted with a nice snowfall.

My older sister, Eleanor, managed to sit nicely while my brothers and I fidgeted and stared out the window longingly. Cousin Jane's betrothed, Mr. Bingley, was a very kind man. We all liked him immediately. He talked and joked with us. His friend, who Mama happily introduced as Mr. Fitzwilliam Darcy, simply sat there, completely still. Well, unless Cousin Lizzy moved. He watched her every movement. She didn't seem to like it either.

"Mr. Darcy," said Lizzy, "although my cousins live in London, they have not had the privilege of visiting the museums. How kind of you to give them a display."

She spoke rather sharply, and he shifted uncomfortably.

"I do not take your meaning, madam."

Such cold politeness!

"You are the exact likeness of a marble statue!"

My mother heard and added to the conversation as Mr. Darcy looked entirely unsure how to reply.

"Oh yes, the Darcys have a very fine gallery of marble. I know there were busts of many of your forefathers. I imagine there is one of you, too, now."

"There is..."

"A very handsome image, I am sure."

"Thank you..."

Was Mr. Darcy blushing?

"I am certain that is what Elizabeth was saying as well."

"Lizzy was saying he was too cold and impersonal!" I felt compelled to correct my mother. Lizzy always said I had her cleverness about me, even if I was only eight years old.

"Kathy!" Eleanor and Lizzy gasped in unison.

"Kathleen," my mother said in the tone that promised I was due serious punishment later. “Take your brothers outside. John can accompany you, so there will be no rough play.”

I frowned. What had I done wrong? We left our governess in London; she was to spend Christmas with her family. John, the Bennet footman, was very large and intimidating.

“I need to check on my horse. I would be happy to oversee the children,” Mr. Darcy suddenly said and stood.

He looked at me intently, and although I was frightened, I would not back down from his glare. When at last he looked away, I glanced towards Lizzy, who was watching Mr. Darcy before she met my eye and winked. I breathed a sigh of relief. Lizzy would ensure Mr. Darcy did us no harm.

I took Matthew and Benjamin in hand and led them outside. Mr. Darcy followed us but stopped to ask the housekeeper a question. A maid appeared to help dress us in our coats and hats, and soon we children were bounding in the wide openness of a country estate.

I entirely forgot about Mr. Darcy’s hateful presence for several minutes as I chased my brothers in play. Then I saw Matthew scoop up a ball of snow and throw it—but not at me. It knocked Mr. Darcy’s hat right off his head. He barely had a chance to react before being pelted in rapid fire with snowballs from behind. Lizzy had snuck out of the house and formed an arsenal of snowballs while we played!

Mr. Darcy spun around in shock—and surely indignation—but a snowball landed squarely on his face. She had no mercy, and as he attempted to wipe off the icy weaponry, she launched another attack. Matthew had joined in by this time, and in another instant, Mr. Darcy's front and back were entirely covered in snow.

I trembled in fear. How angry would he be? But he broke out in a wide grin before scooping up snow and, far too gently, aiming for Lizzy.

She jumped out of the way and teased. "Being a statue again?"

"I am no statue!"

He scooped up a large pile of snow and made a great show of aiming for Lizzy's face. She narrowly ducked out of the way in time. Now that she had engaged her enemy, she was relentless. She lobbed another snowball at him, and he returned it. She ran away again, but now he was no longer content to be stationary. He chased her around, and immediately we children joined in as well. He could not match the four of us, though, and soon we had him on the ground.

"Stop! Stop!" Mr. Darcy pleaded.

Lizzy motioned for us to cease, and she even held out her hand to help him up, although surely such a large man could manage on his own. He took it and pulled her to him, scrambling out of the way as she fell into a heap of snow! What a jolly soul Mr. Darcy had!

"Mr. Darcy!" she shrieked. She laughed at the same time, clearly enjoying the play.

When she caught her breath, she said, "I suppose I deserved that." She looked at Mr. Darcy, covered from head to toe in snow, and chuckled. "We are even now. I am certain I am as bedraggled as you are."

"You are lovelier than ever. A snow nymph." Her hair had tumbled down during all the exercise, and he pushed a stray curl away from her face.

Lizzy's eyes widened. Although her cheeks were already rosy, they became brighter, and she quickly looked away. She hastily stood and dusted herself off, looking around as she did so. I saw her eyes alight on Mr. Darcy's hat, and she brought it back to him.

"Come, children!" she called. "I think we ought to dress up our snowman." She looked at him for a moment in assessment. "He needs a pipe!"

I ran off to the kitchen—we were only a few paces away—and begged for John's old pipe. He parted with it easily when I explained it was for Mr. Darcy.

When I returned, Lizzy was still standing before Mr. Darcy. They were simply staring at each other like a pair of statues now.

"Here! For his pipe." I thrust my cargo into Lizzy's hands.

"Oh!" she exclaimed, finally unfreezing. "Well, let us dress our snowman."

She held up Mr. Darcy's hat, and he had to duck down for her to place it on his head. They both still smiled like fools. She handed him the pipe, and he pretended to take a puff. Then to the amazement of us both, he began to dance a jig.

The boys came running back as they heard us laughing. Lizzy joined Mr. Darcy's dance, but they must have been dizzy from their turning. They nearly bumped into each other, and Mr. Darcy righted Elizabeth before she fell by grasping her waist. He did not let go, however. He hummed a different, slower tune than before. She placed one hand on his shoulder and the other in his hand. They were nearly hugging! Finally, they ceased their steps, but they did not pull apart. White clouds blew rapidly from their mouths, and they looked as though they were out of breath.

Lizzy's cheeks were bright red. "Are you frozen now?" Ben asked.

Mr. Darcy immediately released Lizzy. "Are you cold? Ought we to return to the house?"

With a soft smile, Lizzy answered, "The dancing quite delightfully warmed me. You really ought to dance more."

"If all my dances could be like that, and with you as my partner, I would," he said, and Lizzy drew in a sharp breath.

Mr. Darcy nervously looked away and then up at the sun. "I fear the snow will melt away today; we should enjoy it while we can."

"Chase us!" the boys yelled before scampering off again.

Lizzy pulled me aside, and we came up with a plan.

"Grab a stick, Kathy, and we will be soldiers. Our snowman can be our captain, and we will march to the village!"

Giggling, I ran off to fetch my newest prop, and when I returned, Lizzy and Mr. Darcy had the boys in a straight line. I held up the rear.

"What is our captain's name?" Matthew asked as we began to march.

"He's Fitzywilliam Darcy!" Benjamin cried out.

"Fitzywilliam!" Lizzy choked out between laughs.

"I will have you know, my cousin is a colonel in His Majesty's army—with the Royal Horse Guards Blue—and Fitzwilliam makes a fine name for a military man," Mr. Darcy said with a tone of suppressed laughter.

"Of course..." Lizzy replied. "Or perhaps my cousin meant Frostywilliam. You are still covered in snow, sir."

"As are you, Miss Snow Nymph."

"That I am, Fitzy the Snowman."

We all laughed at Mr. Darcy's new name.

We marched the short distance past the lodge and entered Longbourn village. A few children joined in behind us. Soon we were on our return march, Fitzy the Snowman thrusting his stick up like a baton in time to a jaunty tune Lizzy sang.

Suddenly we came to a halt.

"Darcy!" Mr. Bingley sounded alarmed and walked forward. Two horses trailed behind. "Darcy, Good God! What have you been doing?"

Lizzy broke ranks. "He has been a delightfully entertaining snowman."

Mr. Bingley looked puzzled, but as he glanced from one snow-covered body to the next, a grin broke out on his face.

"I am sorry to have to end your fun, but it is time for us to leave. Darcy you will have to hurry now so you can change if we are to make London before dark."

"You are leaving?" Lizzy turned and asked Mr. Darcy. It sounded like an angry accusation.

"I will be back on Christmas. We are to fetch our sisters for the holiday."

"Oh."

Lizzy suddenly seemed shy, and Mr. Bingley lured us away with promises of warm treats in the kitchen for us. Just before I entered the house, I looked back to Lizzy. Mr. Darcy raised her hand to his lips before mounting his horse. Only I saw her watch after them as the gentlemen left. Their horses galloped over the hill, reminding me of Lizzy's song, but she did not sing this time. She placed the hand he kissed on her cheek.

*****

A few days after we returned to London, we received a letter from Lizzy announcing her betrothal to Mr. Darcy. My parents were surprised, although they had noted Mr. Darcy's attention to Lizzy after his return, but I was not. I knew she fell in love with him the day Fitzy the Snowman came alive.

The End

The Force of Love

Fitzwilliam Darcy sat in his aunt and uncle's drawing room as the family gathered together after the christening of the newest heir to the earldom. Darcy was happy for his cousin Joseph, Viscount Arlington, and his wife, Mary. They had a beautiful daughter about two years ago, and now the heir had arrived. The Biblical connotations of their names were not lost on Darcy or his uncle.

"You know, Joshua is a form of the name Jesus. They both mean Saviour," the earl said.

Joseph laughed. "Yes, Father. We believed no other name would do for the son of Joseph and Mary."

"His birth reminds me of our Saviour's. Our Mary is a very good girl—I could not ask for a better daughter-in-law—but I do not think the Bible's Mary was any more holy than most ladies. I think she was more willing to be used by God, but to make her holier negates Jesus's true divinity."

"I suppose you are right, my Lord," the Viscountess Arlington agreed.

"Nor do I think she had any understanding what bearing the Son of God would truly mean. Could she know that the baby she held in her arms would work miracles? She could not have imagined becoming a Saviour to His people meant sacrificing His life."

Mary looked horrified. "No, no mother can imagine that I am sure."

"I am sure she had no more idea of what He would become in life than you do of your son now."

"He will be raised well, given proper principles. Surely that must mean something," Joseph interjected.

"We may be raised with proper principles but still turn out poorly. How many men of your own position have squandered their youth and fortune, Son?"

Darcy's thoughts turned to his sister, although no one but his other cousin, her co-guardian, knew of her near elopement. "Perhaps it depends on the company one keeps."

"Ha! Then you should be all friendliness instead of arrogance and pride," the viscount replied.

"What do you mean?" He was quite offended.

"You keep company with us, and we are friendly with all of our acquaintances, whereas you are silent and disapproving. Your friend,

Bingley, likely never met a person he could not like in his whole life."

"I am not disapproving."

"You are. You never speak to anyone you are not already acquainted with. For them, you are very forgiving; after all, you tagged along with that Wickham fellow Uncle Darcy paid too much attention to for years. But everyone else must meet your fastidious standards. Tell me, did you make a single friend in Hertfordshire?"

"I do not know how to make myself appear concerned in the affairs of others."

"That is exactly it! You think you must only appear concerned. With all the wealth and power you have, it would be the height of gentlemanly behaviour if you were truly concerned with the affairs of others."

"I feel as though I can little understand the concerns of country gentlemen of little fortune and no consequence."

"Do you hear yourself, Darcy? You are only a gentleman with more land than most. It is not as though you are a peer and focused on Parliament and politics. Irrigation is a pain to everyone just the same." The viscount was clearly growing angry.

"Joseph, Darcy, that is enough," the countess spoke firmly. "I will not have you upsetting my grandson."

"Allow me to say this, my dear," said the earl. "I would hate to be judged only by the offences of my parents. Upbringing is an important factor in any child's life, but there comes a time when they make their own choices. We are all equal in the opportunity for moral success and failure. My parents nearly ruined the estate, but I chose a different path. I believe I raised my sons right, but I do not believe I should be blamed for their failures or given credit for their successes. Joseph is to find his own way in Parliament as an MP now, Richard in the army. Darcy has had to find his own way no matter how good his father was. Georgiana has to choose her path. My sister, Catherine, has chosen hers; now it is up to Anne to follow in the ways of pretension or to act appropriately. Joshua's life is entirely before him; he may do good or evil."

"Hear, hear!" cried the viscount, and Darcy was left to brood in silence as the ladies turned the conversation to things more appropriate following a christening.

That night before falling asleep, Darcy considered the conversation he had with his

family. He considered that if Mary c
how her baby would turn out, then p
did put too much weight on the teac
parents. His parents were good, but they also taught him it was acceptable to be selfish, to care only for himself—something he always knew others did not practice as his cousin and uncle so pointedly displayed this morning. He could not say it was only due to his rearing that he was so stand-offish in company, nor did he have any idea it appeared to others that he disapproved of them.

Perhaps he did disapprove of others, but now it seemed that no one was worthy of his notice. His cousin was correct: he was only a gentleman. Who was he to feel so superior? What merits did he have to himself? His uncle had saved his family from financial ruin, one cousin served in Parliament, and the other in the army. All he did was inherit his father's fortune and responsibilities. He had tried to do well, but he knew he had failed, at least in regards to his sister.

His thoughts turned to Elizabeth Bennet, as they usually did in the evenings. He should not hold her parents and family against her. Perhaps...perhaps it was worth reconsidering a marriage to her. He had spent time enough in

London to know he could not forget her, and indeed he had been in company for many years now. He knew what he desired in a wife, and he knew he had not found it in any other.

He considered, too, his thoughts regarding Jane Bennet—for it would be easier to court Elizabeth from Netherfield, which would mean putting Bingley in Miss Bennet's path once more. Was she truly such a dutiful daughter that she would capitulate to Mrs. Bennet's wishes? Was he perhaps premature in judging the daughter by looking at the mother? And while he could never condone Mrs. Bennet's behaviour, was she so different than his aunt? Were the younger daughters any worse in their flirtatious behaviour than his sister had been by consenting to an elopement?

He thought that if Mary could not have known her son was to become the Messiah, then his parents could not fathom how he, Georgiana, and even Wickham turned out. His parents spoiled them all, and it did them no good. Thinking of Wickham brought to mind another reason he should return to Hertfordshire. He should be concerned for the affairs of the people in the Meryton area, that Wickham could harm them, even if it meant exposing his own affairs.

It was not a requirement of civility, but perhaps it was the most gentlemanly way.

Resolved to return to Hertfordshire and show his newfound humility to the residents, sleep began to claim him peacefully for the first time in weeks. He was blind to his faults but now saw them; he had been deaf to Elizabeth's admonishments but now heard them. He would no longer be mute on Wickham's travesties. Perhaps he could even manage to speak sensibly to Elizabeth and court her good opinion—for he now recognised how poorly she thought of him.

*****

"Father, I have been thinking," Elizabeth heard her sister, Mary, say one day shortly after Christmas. "Before we met Mr. Bingley, you had teased Mama about the importance of proper introductions."

"Yes, what of it?" he replied testily. Any mentions of the Bingleys or Netherfield currently brought on complaints from their mother about Mr. Bingley's continued absence, combined with Elizabeth's rejection of Mr. Collins. Fortunately, Mrs. Bennet was not in the room at the moment.

"How can we know the true character of a gentleman who has no connections in the area?"

"Surely we have seen enough to know Mr. Bingley's amiability," Elizabeth replied.

"Was six weeks enough to learn that? He was most uncivil by not even calling to say goodbye before leaving the area."

"He may still return," Elizabeth said.

"If you believed that, then why would you have encouraged Jane to go to London?"

"Well, his being encouraged to stay by his friends does not mean he is any less amiable."

Mr. Bennet put aside his book. "Now that presents an interesting idea. Perhaps there is such a thing as too amiable. What do you think Lizzy? Mary?"

"A person may lack a certain resolve," Elizabeth said, knowing she had accused Mr. Bingley of that only weeks ago.

"He may have very good reasons for staying in London. Or his friends may, should they truly be encouraging him. I am more interested in the case that we may know a person for quite some time and not truly know them at all. Something I think worth reflecting on with the officers of the militia and their frequency in our home," Mary said while giving pointed looks to Kitty and Lydia.

"Colonel Forster has assured us of the gentlemanliness of every officer," Elizabeth said.

"Mr. Wickham was a new recruit, and Colonel Forster did not know him before he joined the regiment. We have now known Mr. Wickham for about a month, and I daresay all I know is that he hates Mr. Darcy."

"Hates Mr. Darcy? On the contrary, Mr. Wickham has surprising patience and fortitude with Mr. Darcy after how cruelly he has been treated by the man."

"But you only know that because of Mr. Wickham's testimony."

"Which you only knew first because you keep him all to yourself!" Lydia exclaimed from across the room.

"Do not tell me you are crossed in love too, Lizzy," their father teased.

"Hardly, sir."

Mr. Bennet nodded his head in acceptance. "Now, is there truth to Lydia and Mary's claims? You like him so much because Mr. Darcy has slighted the fellow as well?"

Elizabeth felt heat rush to her cheeks. "I only have sympathy for his position. It is not that I commiserate with him for being found unworthy of Mr. Darcy's attentions."

"Ah, but he found you unworthy at first sight and Mr. Wickham he knew all his life. Mr. Wickham tells us that Mr. Darcy was jealous of him. Now, what can possibly be his reasoning for slighting you then?"

"He slighted the entire area! He thinks we are unworthy of his notice!"

"So, why would Wickham accuse Darcy of jealousy when, from what we have seen, it would be more aligned with his character to think Wickham unworthy of the living merely because of his birth?"

Elizabeth stammered, "Mr…Mr. Wickham said there were stronger motives than pride in Mr. Darcy's conduct towards him. I would trust Mr. Wickham to know the truth of their relationship better than we can."

"And yet, can we trust his understanding of the matter?" Mr. Bennet wondered. "Has there not been a recent occurrence that made you doubt your ability to understand a long-time acquaintance?"

Mrs. Bennet then returned to the room, and she began complaining about how the Lucases misused her with their designs on Mr. Collins. As Elizabeth returned to her chamber that evening, she meditated on her father's questions. She was surprised that her best friend would marry Mr. Collins for nothing more than mercenary reasons. It *must* be called such. If she truly worried so much for her future security, then she might have married one of the local men. Their area lacked men of much independent means, and however odious Mr. Collins was, he currently held a valuable living and would one day inherit Longbourn. His position was better than many of the gentlemen Elizabeth had met, and Charlotte was no fool.

If Elizabeth misunderstood Charlotte, might Mr. Wickham have misunderstood Mr. Darcy? She could not absolve him of denying Mr. Wickham his due; she had no reason to think well of him. It was possible Mr. Wickham was too close to the situation to see it clearly. Mr. Darcy's first and last motive in every action must be his pride. And yet...she recalled her questioning of Mr. Wickham on the very subject. By all she understood of Mr. Darcy, he ought to have too much pride to deal dishonestly with Mr. Wickham. Still more, she wondered how such a picture of Mr. Darcy could be true, and yet he could be friends with Mr. Bingley. She found herself declaring contradictions of each man and barely slept.

Despite the cold of late December weather, Elizabeth took her customary walk the next morning. As she walked into Meryton, she saw Mr. Wickham talking with a group of young ladies. After a moment, he extended his arm towards one lady in particular, a Miss King, and they proceeded in her direction. When they saw her, instead of delaying to speak, Mr. Wickham only coloured slightly and then nodded his head. Miss King tightened her hold on Mr. Wickham's arm while smiling up at him. Elizabeth could hardly make sense of the scene. Mr. Wickham almost looked guilty at being seen by her with Miss King, and yet she could not understand what would elicit that feeling. Elizabeth did not know Miss King well, but they had always been friendly before. She could not think of a reason for Mr. Wickham to feel as though his allegiance was divided.

"How strange that I care little for the lack of attention he gave me and am instead intrigued by the curiosity of the scene," she said to herself. "How many other ladies might be jealous that he walked with another lady?" She shrugged her shoulders but kept her eyes on the ground, avoiding the puddles a recent rain left. "It is as I said to my aunt. I am most definitely not in love with him."

"Pity the man who does not have Miss Elizabeth Bennet's love," an unexpected voice startled her.

"Oh!" she cried and looked up just before colliding with Mr. Darcy. She began to fall backwards, and as she threw an arm out to steady herself, Mr. Darcy grasped her hand and pulled her forward. Momentum did the rest, and she slammed into Mr. Darcy's chest. "Ooomph!" She blushed in embarrassment.

"Are you well? I did not mean to startle you," he said, and his deep voice rumbled in her ear. Why was she still against him? She immediately took a step backwards, only then realising that Mr. Darcy had wrapped his arms around her.

Confused, she stammered a reply. "I am uninjured. I am sorry to have inconvenienced you." She turned to go around him when she suddenly realised the strangeness that he was in Hertfordshire and wondered if Mr. Bingley had returned. "I thought you were in London! It is quite unexpected to see you here!"

"I returned to Netherfield just last night. I mean to call on Longbourn later in the morning but am glad to have found you alone."

Elizabeth cared little for his words and instead peered around him. "I know my family will be quite pleased to see the return of the Netherfield party. That is, all but Jane can be pleased as she is in London. Do Mr. Bingley's sisters remain there? I know Jane intends to call on them."

"Might we speak candidly, Miss Bennet?"

She looked at him appraisingly. "We can try."

"As I said in our last conversation, I am aware that you may have been given untruthful information to make you distrust me. At the time, I asked that you not sketch my character, and you claimed it may be your last chance. If your study is not complete, then I would give you another opportunity now."

His offer was too tempting. If he had arrived yesterday, she likely would have had no reason to amend her thoughts on him, but the conversation from the day before had altered her opinion of her own judgment. "If we are to continue our acquaintance, it is only correct that I would keep an open mind regarding you."

Mr. Darcy smiled slightly. "I will take that as a yes." He led her on the path towards Netherfield. "Miss Bingley and Mrs. Hurst did not accompany their brother to Netherfield. They wish to enjoy the Season, and he hoped to experience the house during the winter. He claims London holds no interest for him. How does your sister enjoy her time in Town?"

Elizabeth raised her eyebrows in surprise. It seemed that Mr. Darcy was asking about Jane's preference for Mr. Bingley. "My aunt and uncle frequently invite Jane and me to stay with them in Town. I do not think she would have agreed this winter, however, if not for one particular reason."

"Yes, you said that she plans to call on Miss Bingley. She must not wish for her friendship to be interrupted."

Elizabeth carefully weighed her next words. "It is true that Jane enjoyed Miss Bingley's friendship. I have never seen her happier than when she expected to see her Netherfield friends at events in Hertfordshire. However, she is aware that my aunt and uncle do not frequently go out in Town and have such different circles of friends that frequently seeing any of her newest acquaintances is unlikely. In truth, the environs of Hertfordshire, memories provoked, and the gossiping inhabitants thereof seemed to pain her. She left for London in very dejected spirits."

She looked at Mr. Darcy, who at first looked surprised but quickly hid his reaction.

"What part of my statement surprised you? That we are aware of my aunt and uncle's position in life? It surprises you that one might neither be haughty nor obsequious?"

"I would never accuse you of such a thing. I suggested a frankness in our conversation to which you were hesitant to agree, but I will show you my commitment to it. I was surprised that your sister was capable of such strong feelings. I mistook what I believe now must be general reserve for indifference. I imagined it possible that she followed Mr. Bingley to London, but rather to learn that she went to London to *avoid* seeing him and memories of him has shocked me."

The man was too honest for his own good! She easily saw by his expression that he thought he should be praised for his scruples. "With your pleased countenance at confessing to deriding my sister, I wonder how you dare to be so dishonest towards Mr. Wickham."

"You take an eager interest in that man's affairs!"

"Who that calls him friend can help but be interested in his misfortunes?"

"Misfortunes indeed!"

"What do you call it when a man is deprived his only means for support? When it is done by design?"

"I have deprived him by design? I understand by your words he has told you that I did not give him a living meant for him, suggested by my father?"

"He told me you disqualified him because he spoke too openly of his poor opinion of you."

"He gave up the living!" Mr. Darcy roared, causing her to jump. He paced in front of her but spoke in a calmer voice. "When my father died, Wickham gave up the living. He was to study the law, and I gave him an additional three thousand pounds. He lived in dissipation for three years, and when he heard the living was vacant, he asked for it anyway. I refused, and he had no scruples about verbally abusing me. That is when *his* design began."

Elizabeth listened in disbelieving astonishment as Mr. Darcy told her that Wickham had met with Darcy's fifteen-year-old sister and convinced her of an elopement all in an effort to gain her impressive dowry.

"No, it cannot be," she said when he finished.

"What reason would I have to lie?"

"You...you cannot bear for others to think lowly of you!"

"If I were truly proud and haughty, would I care what you or Meryton thought of me?"

"Well..." She searched her mind for a quick answer and found none. "If what you say is true, why do you share it with me?"

"I intend to make it known to your father and as many people in the area as I can. Mr. Wickham is not to be trusted."

"You would give up your sister's reputation?"

"I do not think that will be necessary with the others."

"Then why tell me?"

He took a step closer to her and spoke gently. "I trust you. You have asked to know my character when others see only the worth of my name and income."

She had thought he disliked that about her. Before she could reply, they heard steps and turned to look at the intruder.

"Darcy! Miss Elizabeth! How nice to see you!" Mr. Bingley jovially called out.

After she assured Mr. Bingley how pleased she was to learn of his return to the area, he said, "Darcy and I were to call on Longbourn later this morning to visit your parents and sisters. Are *all* your sisters still at Longbourn?"

"Jane is currently in London visiting my aunt and uncle."

"London! To think we never heard of her being there. Did you, Darcy?" Without allowing his friend to answer, he turned back to Elizabeth. "I suppose she just recently arrived then?"

Elizabeth saw Mr. Darcy looked quite conscious and decided it was between them how much he had kept from his friend. Elizabeth knew Jane had written Miss Bingley of her arrival in London. It was clear that Mr. Bingley did not know of Jane's presence, but Darcy had shown no surprise when Elizabeth mentioned Jane being in London. She rather wondered if Miss Bingley had mentioned it to Darcy. "She returned with them about a week ago."

"But do you know how long she means to be there?"

"I do not, sir."

Mr. Bingley looked pained with indecision. Darcy spoke. "Perhaps your sisters may know more when you return to retrieve them in a few days."

"But..." he trailed off as Darcy gave him a meaningful look. "Oh yes! Yes, I will be returning to London, only to fetch Caroline, Louisa, and Hurst, later this week. They could not quite part with…" Seemingly realising he was rambling, he ceased speaking.

An awkward silence descended upon the three of them until, at last, Elizabeth spoke. "I should return for breakfast. I look forward to your call."

She quickly said goodbye and scurried away. Exerting herself as much as she could on the way home so she could not spare thoughts on the strange morning and her argument with Mr. Darcy, she arrived home out of breath and with rosy cheeks.

"Lizzy! You will never believe what our aunt Phillips told us while you were gone!" Lydia ran to her side immediately.

"What?" she said while untying her bonnet and attempting to calm her racing heart.

"Miss King has—" Kitty began but was interrupted.

"No! You do not tell it well!" Lydia interjected. "Miss King's grandfather finally died, and she inherited ten thousand pounds! Aunt Phillips said she was wearing a dress in London's latest fashion this morning, surrounded by beaus, and smiling as though she were a painted peacock. They can only want her money; she has all those nasty freckles! It is just as well that a man can get something out of marriage to her for gaining such an ugly wife!"

A chill ran up Elizabeth's spine. Mr. Wickham's guilty look this morning was because she had caught him transferring his attentions to Miss King for want of her inheritance. If he could be so mercenary as to attach himself to a lady of merely ten thousand pounds, then what would he do for one with that of Miss Darcy's worth?

Elizabeth paled and stumbled towards the stairs.

"Lizzy? Are you well?" Mary asked.

"Perfectly. I just need to refresh myself after my walk."

Upon reaching her room, she sat on her bed. What a blind fool she had been! She had thought she was perfectly sensible about Mr. Wickham and Mr. Darcy. *Wretched vanity!* Flattered by Mr. Wickham's attention and offended by Mr. Darcy's first estimation of her, she allowed herself to be prejudiced at every turn with both of them.

She soon thought of what Mr. Darcy had said of Jane and Bingley. He believed Jane indifferent to Bingley. Even Charlotte thought Jane displayed her feelings too little. She owed

Mr. Darcy a hearty apology and, still more, wondered how Bingley and Jane could soon meet again. Resolved to try and gain a moment alone with Mr. Darcy, she awaited him and Bingley outside.

They arrived on their mounts at the usual calling time. Mr. Bingley was all easiness at seeing her again, but Darcy stood back. After a few pleasantries with Bingley, Elizabeth gathered her courage. "If you will excuse us, I wondered if Mr. Darcy and I might finish our conversation from earlier." She trusted Bingley would not feel slighted, and indeed he did not. He happily agreed to go ahead to the house.

"Mr. Darcy," Elizabeth began once they were alone, "I apologise for my intemperate response to your information earlier. I believe it was kindly meant. I have since reflected on your words and trust the merit of them. The truth is," she took a deep breath before continuing, "I have been prejudiced towards you, and my dislike of you gave me a false impression of Mr. Wickham. If you can forgive my impertinence, might we start fresh as new acquaintances?"

He took a moment before replying, and Elizabeth began to expect his wrath. Instead, he said in an affected voice, "I can easily forgive you as I regret my own mode of approach. My manners and expressions merited reproach, and even after, I came to the conclusion that I have treated the whole of Meryton badly."

"You cannot be so harsh upon yourself. You might have offended others at first, but I believe I have been the only person to never give you any credit and to have refused to alter my original perceptions of you. But you should learn some of my philosophy: remember the past only as its remembrance gives you pleasure."

"It is not philosophy that can give you such contentment but rather your innocence. You had every right to think that I would scheme to separate your sister from my friend for my own motives. I gave you every cause to think Wickham's accusations were truthful. I have been tortured for weeks now with the realisation that you thought lowly of me the entire time I was in Hertfordshire. I believe I have learned my lesson now."

Elizabeth could hardly comprehend his gallantry at making her so entirely blameless. "I cannot recall the events you reference. You must have me confused with someone else." Truthfully, it was as though she was seeing him for the first time, and since she no longer acted under prejudice, she was likely a new person to him as well.

He smiled and played along. "My apologies."

She directed him towards the house. "Will you be returning to London with Mr. Bingley?"

"Yes, I can only spare a few days here. I came after having reason to wonder if your sister truly did care for Bingley and to deliver my warning about Wickham. I should speak to your father now."

Just before entering Longbourn, they stepped under a mistletoe ball still left hanging. Darcy looked up.

"We have been slow to take our decorations down, as you see." She felt herself blush but could not fathom it being because Darcy might kiss her.

He stepped closer to her and reached for a berry over her head. "Nonsense, it is only just after Twelfth Night." His breath fanned her cheek, and inexplicably, her heart rate increased.

"Do the rules still apply after the holiday?"

His eyes searched hers. "The rules?"

"That a gentleman must kiss any lady he finds under the bough and that she will be unlucky in love if she refuses."

"It would be a shame to be unlucky in love. Would you really want to risk it?"

She smiled at his tease. “You talk as though you truly mean to—”

His lips met hers, and all thought left her mind. For one delicious moment, reason, wit, and residual resentment died away, and only she and Mr. Darcy existed. When she opened her eyes, he was gone, and Elizabeth was left wondering if she had imagined the entire encounter.

*****

Despite the fact that Elizabeth believed the entire world shifted on its axis in early January when Mr. Darcy returned with Mr. Bingley, Hertfordshire society continued on with little change. Mr. Bingley and Mr. Darcy returned to London as planned. While there, Mr. Bingley renewed his acquaintance with Jane, and when Bingley again stayed in Town longer than expected, Elizabeth found she could *almost* be happy with his pliancy. Only the realisation that she was in agreement with her mother in wishing that Bingley would court Jane from Netherfield forced Elizabeth to calm her nerves. Instead, she contended herself with reading accounts of Mr. Darcy’s behaviour in letters from Jane. She never saw anything that made her believe he thought of her at all. Jane made no mention of him asking after Elizabeth. Her aunt's letters said little more than how excessively civil he was to them all, taking pains for them to meet his sister and inviting them to dinner at his house.

January lapsed to February, and at last Elizabeth would be going to London before travelling onward to Hunsford to visit her friend, the newly married Mrs. Collins. They would only be in Town for a day, and she could hardly hope to meet Mr. Darcy in such a small span of time. Upon arriving at the Gardiner residence and hearing that they would attend the theatre in Mr. Darcy's box, she could scarcely contain her delight.

"We shall be seeing Twelfth Night. Mr. Darcy said he thought you might enjoy it. I hope you do, although I do not recall you ever saying you preferred it much before," Mrs. Gardiner said to them in the carriage.

Twelfth Night! Could he be thinking of their last encounter still? They arrived in due time, and Mr. Darcy awaited them in the hall. Mr. Bingley and his sisters were there as well. Bingley immediately went to Jane's side, but Miss Bingley remained perched on Mr. Darcy's arm. Elizabeth hardly knew what she hoped to learn from the evening even without the presence of Miss Bingley, but now any chance of private conversation was impossible.

They soon went up to his box but before sitting were met by a very amiable older gentleman and elegant lady with the appearance of rank. Darcy introduced them as his aunt and uncle, the Earl and Countess of Matlock. Seeing their large party, they mentioned the open seats they had in their own box. Miss Bingley and the Hursts eagerly agreed to sit with them, and Elizabeth smiled in wonder as Darcy sat her to his left.

The play began before she found courage to speak. She forced herself to seem calm when she wished to wring her hands in distraction. It was some time towards the end of the first act when she felt a tap on her hand.

"Forgive me, I ought to have asked earlier," Darcy said. "I have an extra opera glass should you wish to use it."

"Thank you," Elizabeth said. When she reached for them, Darcy pressed a Christmas rose into her hand along with the glass. She looked at him in confusion.

"For when we meet again in Kent. I was out of mistletoe." He squeezed her hand and then put the bloom above her ear. His hand grazed her face as he lowered it. "Even lovelier."

The play could no longer hold Elizabeth's attention as her thoughts rapidly swirled in her mind. It had been plainly in front of her all the time, and she refused to see it. In the months since their last meeting, she had plenty of time to review their every encounter. Where she once catalogued Darcy's every fault, she now saw only his strength of character and honour. Could logic so thoroughly acquit him of every evil? No, the greater force of love was to blame.

Elizabeth impatiently awaited for his arrival at Rosings. They met by chance on a walk by an oak tree. Weeks later when it was time for Darcy to depart, he proposed marriage under the same tree. Elizabeth accepted with all of her heart. When their eldest daughter was born near Christmas day two years later, the couple agreed she ought to be named Mary Anne, for without the words of relatives named Mary they may never have met again.

The End

Home with You

"Jane, are you coming with us to town?" Kitty asked her eldest sister. "We want to see the officers."

"You will see them this evening at dinner," Elizabeth chided.

"Well, I wish to speak with Mr. Wickham, and we can never do that if you are there," Lydia reprimanded, and Elizabeth blushed.

It was true; he paid his attentions quite obviously to Elizabeth. It could only remind Jane of her own pain.

"She will not come. She wants to sit and pine over Mr. Bingley," Lydia said in a very teasing and unsympathetic tone.

"Hush." Elizabeth shooed her sisters from Jane's side, and they loudly went down the stairs to question if Mary would join them. "Have you thought, dearest, about returning to London with Aunt and Uncle?"

Jane smiled a little. "You think I might see Mr. Bingley there?"

Elizabeth frowned. "I do not think so. It does not seem likely that Miss Bingley would encourage such a meeting, but you would be away from Mama and her incessant complaints.

Town has many diversions, and I know you enjoy the company of the Gardiners and their children."

Jane nodded. "Yes, I suppose it would be enjoyable."

Elizabeth squeezed her hands and left the room. Their mother was insisting that she accompany Kitty and Lydia to Meryton. Since she recently refused an offer of marriage to Mr. Collins, the estate's heir, her mother was attempting to push Elizabeth into the arms of any willing man.

For a moment, Jane felt jealousy. She had never received an offer of marriage, but how could she be jealous of Elizabeth's very unwanted offer from a man such as Mr. Collins? Still, it was no secret that she had hopes of receiving one from Mr. Bingley. Their mother had assumed as much from many gentlemen over the years, but he was the first one Jane actually wished and hoped for.

Aside from Mr. Bingley's departure from the neighbourhood and the clear intent of his sister to never have him return, Jane felt increasingly lonely. Elizabeth had never found a man to stir her interest. Well, at least not romantically; she certainly was interested in smearing Mr. Darcy's name. She could not understand Jane's pain, no matter how empathetic she tried to be. Jane's other good friend, Charlotte Lucas, had just become betrothed to the very Mr. Collins whom Elizabeth had refused. Charlotte had no romantic expectations, and Jane had the sense that Charlotte found both Elizabeth and herself entirely insensible. Surely Charlotte thought Elizabeth should have accepted Mr. Collins, and she likely thought Jane should have done something to attach Mr. Bingley. Charlotte certainly must have done something to attach Mr. Collins so quickly for he proposed to her less than three days after proposing to Elizabeth. But that thought was uncharitable, and taking it in the best light was simply that Charlotte and Mr. Collins were well-suited to each other and would be happy.

Still, she had no friends who could understand. The bells would ring at the churches on Christmas in only a few days, and nothing would alleviate her melancholy. She missed Mr. Bingley; she would miss him for a lifetime.

She cared nothing for the reverent songs of the season. The only song in her heart wished Mr. Bingley back to Netherfield for Christmas.

That afternoon, her aunt and uncle Gardiner arrived. Mrs. Bennet was all aflutter.

"Oh! You arrived so late that I was certain you had been attacked by highwaymen!"

"Hardly likely, my dear," Mr. Bennet said.

"Or that you had changed your mind!"

"Now why would we do that?" Mr. Gardiner asked. "Christmas is a time to visit family and be with the ones you love."

Jane tried not to sniff.

The Gardiners were soon settled, and Jane was rushed off to get ready for the evening. She could not enjoy the dinner or subsequent entertainment at all. Her mother loudly complained about the loss of Mr. Bingley, increasing Jane's every feeling of grief and pain.

She and Elizabeth had never discussed it. She would never have had the words before, but now she would say she knew that she truly loved Mr. Bingley because she felt a physical emptiness without him. She had fantasised about being engaged by Christmas and visiting Netherfield as its future mistress. She was uncertain she could ever have a happy Christmas again.

On Christmas morning, she arose and blindly readied herself for the day. Her ever-present serene demeanour entirely hid the truth of how she felt. Cold, alone, dull to anything but loneliness. She followed her family into the church and went through the motions, not noticing all the whispers and the pointed glances between her and some figure in the back. She was hauled out of her seat by her mother the minute the service was over and nearly launched into the arms of a man. Gasping, she looked up into the eyes of Mr. Bingley!

She burst into tears. "You came home for Christmas!"

He fervently nodded, placed her hand on his arm, and led her away from the throng of people—all staring in their direction.

"Darcy forgot a book, and I was only to write the housekeeper and ask her to send it on, but I decided to come myself. Christmas is a time to be with those you love."

She had been looking at her hands but jerked her head up to meet his eyes. "You love me?"

"Yes, I do."

She broke into a wide grin. "Oh! What a happy Christmas!"

He chuckled but looked earnestly at her. "Dare I hope you return my sentiments?"

At first she could not speak. She only smiled and nodded. "Yes, I do. Now tell me that you will never leave me alone at Christmas again."

"Never again."

Over the course of their long marriage, Charles Bingley kept his pledge. Christmas was not always celebrated at their house. More than one Christmas was spent at Longbourn overlooking the grating behaviour of Mrs. Bennet and the younger girls, but if Jane was with him, he always found his home.

The End

Fortune Favours the Bold

Charles Bingley walked down the fashionable section of Bond Street alone. His sisters were shopping, and his brother-in-law was at his club. Georgiana had a cold, and Darcy clucked over her as a mother hen, refusing to leave the house. It was just as well; solitude let him dwell on happy memories in the company of his one true love. She was indifferent to him—Darcy would only speak the truth and would never wish to wound him—but it could not change his own feelings. When he left for London the day after hosting a ball, he needed to meet with his solicitor. While there, he began arrangements for a marriage settlement, but then his sisters and Darcy arrived with the depressing truth. Even if he wished to marry an indifferent lady—which he did not—she would do nothing for his family's advancement. If she had even liked him, it would be worth it all, but as it was...

He glanced around him and saw a young buck with a lady on his arm. A matronly sister trailed behind. The gentleman directed the ladies to a jewellery shop, and the one on his arm exclaimed in delight. That was precisely how he had expected to spend Christmas this year. He had always enjoyed buying gifts for those he loved but had planned to shower Jane to express what he could not say with words. Now he was left wandering the cold alone, hoping to numb his heart. If only he could see her one last time.

He began to wonder what he would say. If he were speaking to her as though it were the end of their acquaintance, then he would hope that at least she had some happy memories of their conversations. Something that might cheer her when she was melancholy, like the thought of her gentle smile and soft-spoken words did for him.

Other men would talk themselves out of his next thought, but he decided to send her an anonymous note, simply wishing her a happy Christmas. He returned directly to Hurst's townhouse and wrote:

I wish you a merry Christmas.

He hesitated and then finished with:

I know I am dreadfully breaking propriety, but I wanted to tell you I care. I hope you can guess who this is from.

A few blocks away, another Christmas note was written. Georgiana Darcy had sent her brother on an errand so she would have time to write her letter to Miss Elizabeth Bennet.

Forgive the impertinence, but I cannot help but wonder about how Christmas is celebrated in your home. My brother tells me you have four sisters; it must be so joyous to share the holiday with so many loved ones. I have only my brother and must thank you for bringing some kind of cheer to him.

William wrote of you in letters. I have a terrible cold, and while he watches over me, he tells me frequently of something he learned when you were at Netherfield nursing your sister. You may imagine that after the loss of our parents, Christmas has been a sad time for us, but William is now more willing to find the joy in the season. For your kindness to my brother and me, I thank you. I wish you a happy Christmas.

Georgiana sealed it and had her maid send it out for the post directly before she could think better of writing to a total stranger.

*****

Jane stared at the letter in her hand. She thought she recognised the writing.

"Who is it from?" Mrs. Bennet wanted to know.

"Probably Miss Bingley again," said Kitty.

"No, that was not her handwriting. Rather ungraceful, but it was postmarked from London." Mrs. Bennet was insistent as she tried to peer over her daughter's shoulder.

"For Heaven's sake, madam. It must be Mrs. Hurst then. Now leave the girl alone." Mr. Bennet finally interceded before getting up from the breakfast table and returning to his library sanctuary.

As soon as she could, Jane went upstairs to read her letter. She thought she would weep and knew there was only one thing she could do. As she gathered her writing materials, Elizabeth entered the room.

"Jane, I have received the most curious letter."

"I did not know you got one."

"Oh yes. Mama was so interested in yours and any news of Mr. Bingley that she paid no attention to me at all."

"Well, what did yours say?"

Elizabeth handed her the letter, and Jane's eyes went wide. "My, dear Lizzy! Mr. Darcy must be in love with you!"

"That is silly! He could not talk to me without contempt, and he is gone from the area. That hardly speaks to admiration."

"I am surprised to hear you think so as often as you have told me Mr. Bingley loves me although he is not here."

"It is different for you entirely! Mr. Bingley paid you so much attention that only a blind person could think he was not in love with you."

"He *is* in love with me."

"I am so glad to hear you admit it! And without sorrow, too. What has changed?"

"He wrote me a letter," Jane said softly.

"What?"

"Here." She handed her letter to Elizabeth.

"You must write him back! Care not for propriety. Write him every week until he returns in case that nasty sister of his steals the letter."

"You think she would be so awful?"

"I am certain she would."

"I do not know if I have courage enough to write so many letters. He may love me now but have forgotten me by the time he reads it."

"Do you really think he is as fickle as that?"

"No, but it is a fear I have nevertheless."

"Cease speaking and write."

"I will—only if you reply to your own letter."

"Oh, why would I want to correspond with Miss Darcy?"

"She certainly does not seem to be the proud and ill-natured young lady Mr. Wickham told you about."

"I suppose not."

"It really was unfair of him to speak of a person we have no acquaintance with and cannot form our own opinion of."

"That may be, but we all know Mr. Darcy, and Mr. Wickham's assessment of him is quite correct."

"Is it? Do we really know him? For some we may know off a few days acquaintance, others are more difficult to sketch. If he would lie about Miss Darcy, why not lie about the brother?"

"That is the most unforgiving speech I have heard you utter in your entire life."

"It is simple. I believe Mr. Darcy in love with you, and I am not blind to his good qualities. If there is any chance at all that you may return his feelings, then I am very angry at someone who may interfere, having lived through it myself."

"Mr. Darcy is the last man in the world I could ever love!"

"Will you promise me that if you meet with him again you will try and begin a new acquaintance with him? Befriend him free of prejudice."

"Me, prejudiced! He is the one who believes we are not worth his notice because we are so far below him."

"I have heard enough, Lizzy. Shall I write my letter or not? For it depends on if you write one as well."

"Very well," Elizabeth said with remorse.

Jane smiled and set to work on her own letter as Elizabeth returned to the drawing room to write one as well.

*****

Two days later, Bingley was announced at Darcy House.

"Darcy, I am returning to Netherfield. I thought I might extend the invitation to you and Georgiana to go with me."

Before Darcy could reply, Georgiana jumped up from her seat. "Oh, please! Let us go."

"I cannot imagine why you are so excited," Darcy said, clearly unexcited himself.

"I...I have corresponded with Miss Elizabeth Bennet. I would like to meet her."

"You have done what?"

Georgiana raised her chin. “I wrote a note to thank her for befriending you in Hertfordshire. You had so many stories to tell about her in your letters and since you have been home. You laugh more often now, too, and smile sometimes for no reason. You have been very unhappy since...the summer.”

“Darcy and Miss Elizabeth friends? No, all they do is argue!” Bingley cried.

“We debate. It is what civilised and intelligent people do.”

Georgiana met Bingley’s eye and raised her eyebrows. A slow smile crossed his face. Perhaps Bingley could not debate many matters, but he understood the social cues of people far better than her brother could. They both agreed that Darcy was besotted.

Knowing her brother could refuse her nothing, she pressed her point, and at length a returned trip was planned two days hence. Bingley directed the carriage to Longbourn. Luck had it that Jane and Elizabeth were out of doors when the carriage arrived, or perhaps it was due to the letters they both received indicating the expected arrival time of their guests.

Georgiana easily overheard Bingley speaking with Miss Bennet. “I had to come straight to you to wish you a happy Christmas.”

She smiled brilliantly in return.

Georgiana was eager herself to speak with Miss Elizabeth but waited for her brother to introduce them.

"I have so looked forward to meeting you, Miss Elizabeth," she said.

"And I you. Your letter was most surprising."

"I hope you do not mind. I know it is poor manners to write unacquainted, but I felt I owed you too much."

Elizabeth blushed. "Oh, I am certain you far overestimate me and give me too much credit."

Before she could speak, Darcy replied, "And I am equally certain she did not."

Elizabeth raised an eyebrow, and her eyes twinkled. "So you read her letter? Then you know all the terrible secrets of your youth that she passed on to me!"

Her brother's colour drained from his face for a moment, and Georgiana was shocked, but he soon recovered.

"I recall that you dearly love a laugh and to plague and tease."

"I must find some way to win our argument, and I am not above fighting unfairly."

"You have won our debate, Miss Elizabeth. You debate amongst equals."

Elizabeth looked at him for a long minute before beaming. Jane and Bingley were turning into the house, and Darcy offered an arm to each remaining lady.

It surprised all but three in attendance at Sir William Lucas's Christmas dance when during a game involving a kissing bough, the music ceased just as Darcy and Elizabeth were underneath it. Of course, Georgiana had been invited to play. If her matchmaking schemes were guessed by her brother and Miss Elizabeth, they seemed far too pleased with the after-effects of their kiss to comment on it.

The following Christmas, no letters were required between the parties as they were all in residence at Netherfield. Some years they celebrated at Pemberley, and others at the new Bingley estate—less than thirty miles away—but they always celebrated together.

The End

Winter Walks

Darcy and Elizabeth walked hand in hand through the snowy lanes around Longbourn. Jane and Bingley walked a quarter of a mile behind them. There had been an early snow, and now the whole countryside looked magical. In the distance, one could hear sleigh bells and children laughing. It was a perfect time for an engagement period.

Sometimes they talked, and sometimes they enjoyed a companionable silence, their feelings too much to speak.

"Oh, look! What a lovely bird!" Elizabeth exclaimed and broke the silence. "Do you know it?"

Darcy broke his gaze from her lovely face. He loved watching her. All of her emotions were so clearly written on her face and in her eyes. He looked towards where she pointed.

"No, my interests have never turned towards birds except for some knowledge of falconry."

"I confess I do not know many breeds either. I did once read of a beautiful bird found in Africa. They named it a lovebird because it was very faithful and mated only with one bird."

She blushed a little as she realised she spoke of mating.

He caught her eye and spoke lowly. "Will you be my lovebird then, Elizabeth?"

It was so hard to keep her wits about her when he spoke like that and looked at her like that. How had she ever thought it was disapproval? "Of course," she replied. Then gathering her senses some, added, "I am already, am I not?"

"Hmmm," was his only reply.

"Or do you feel compelled to propose again? By all means, continue asking, for though I am a woman, I will prove to you my constancy." There, that should be a fair amount of teasing on the subject.

He made no reply and instead squeezed her hand. They resumed walking in silence for some time, although it felt entirely different than before, until they came upon a snowman.

Some children must have made him up. They even wrapped a scarf around him and placed a hat on his head. For some reason, he reminded her of their old parson. He had always worn an old red scarf like the one on the snowman. She playfully leaned her head towards him as though he were speaking to her.

"What is that, Mr. Hughes? Oh, no, we are not married yet. Of course, you can perform the ceremony!"

Darcy approached her side. "You are so willing to put off our marriage that you want a snowman to perform it?"

At first she hoped he was teasing, but a look at his face showed his vulnerable expression. "No, it is that I am so eager for our marriage, and he is here, instead of waiting another two weeks."

His face broke out in a grin, and he came closer to her side. "Well, I do have the special licence. We could marry today."

The look in his eye convinced Elizabeth that he would love nothing more. It was tempting, but poor Mama...her thoughts ceased as he kissed her.

It was not their first, but they had not been able to indulge very often either. Just when she was losing herself entirely, he pulled back. Yes, very tempting to marry today indeed!

"Your nose is cold," he chuckled.

"Then you should warm it again."

"Lizzy," he said lowly, and she thrilled when he kissed her again.

Finally, he broke the kiss, and when they were calmed, he pulled on her hand to walk back to Longbourn. Glancing over his shoulder, he said, "He looks more like Sir William Lucas to me."

Elizabeth broke out into laughter. The sweet man always kept her guessing.

Later that evening, they sipped coffee before the fire and spoke more of their post-wedding plans. It was daunting, but together they found the strength to hold fast to their original wedding date. If nothing else, their honeymoon plans would have been altered, and Darcy House would have been unprepared for its mistress. Spending their wedding night at Longbourn or Netherfield was much more terrifying than two more weeks of Mrs. Bennet's wedding plans. In the meantime, there would be winter walks.

The End

Darcy's Christmas Wish

A Pride and Prejudice Variation

by

PENELOPE SWAN

EXCERPT

Fifteen years ago...

"You will come and sit here next to me, Fitzwilliam."

Fitzwilliam Darcy got up reluctantly and eyed his aunt, Lady Catherine de Bourgh, with slight apprehension. It was not that he was scared of her, exactly, but she was an intimidating woman, with her tall, imposing figure and flashing dark eyes. She had a loud voice and a way of looking down her long nose at people which made one feel nervous and insignificant. He glanced across at his mother, with her pretty, soft face and her gentle manners. Sometimes he wondered how Lady Catherine and his mother could really be sisters—the only thing they seemed to share were their dark hair and high, arched eyebrows!

Still... Darcy straightened his shoulders. He was nearly twelve years old now and his father had said that it was time he began to conduct himself like a gentleman. He could still remember the recent discourse his father had given him on the subject:

"A gentleman must at all times be courteous and considerate to others, particularly towards the ladies. It is not merely enough to be well-bred—a true gentleman must be of both good birth and noble character, always willing to fulfil his obligations and behave according to the highest ideals of chivalry and personal integrity."

Furthermore, his father had emphasised that to take his place as a gentleman in society, Darcy would have to learn the niceties of social conduct, including, occasionally, enduring conversation and company which was not necessarily pleasing to him. Naturally, his father had hastened to add, this was not required if he was among strangers or those of inferior social class, but with his own family and those of similar consequence he must take the trouble to make himself agreeable.

Thus, Darcy pinned a polite smile on his face and walked across the salon to Lady Catherine, who gestured to the sofa next to her. Darcy sat down obediently in the space indicated—next to his cousin, Anne, who gave a delicate little cough into the lace handkerchief she held in her hands. Her governess hurriedly placed a shawl around her shoulders and fussed over her charge as Darcy shifted uncomfortably next to them.

Anne sneezed and dropped her handkerchief, which fluttered to the floor. Darcy bent over to retrieve it and as he straightened and handed it to his cousin, he caught his aunt eyeing him with a speculative gleam in her eyes. She leaned across to his mother and nodded smugly.

"There, you see, Anne? Behold how well they suit each other. I knew it would be a good match! Have we not always planned this union from the cradle?"

Darcy shifted even more uncomfortably. He hated the way his aunt was always talking about him and Anne, wriggling her eyebrows and smiling in that meaningful way. Father had laughed and told him not to take the comments to heart but it was difficult to ignore them when Lady Catherine seemed to talk of nothing else.

Marry Anne? Darcy glanced surreptitiously at his cousin. He could not imagine being married to anyone. That was something that grown-ups did and even though Father had said that he was now no longer a boy but on the way to becoming a man, marriage still seemed too far away to even think about.

Besides... he glanced at his cousin again. What a bore it would be having Anne for a wife! He would certainly not wish to spend his life with someone so pale and insipid. She never said anything, except for the occasional whisper in answer to her governess's question about whether she was too hot or too cold, or had too much or too little light on her... Darcy did not really know what he should like in a wife but he knew it would not be someone like Anne.

No, I'd like someone fun, he thought. *Someone who enjoys reading like I do and who can talk about anything, not just silly girls' stuff... someone who'd come exploring with me in the woods and we could have adventures together and climb up—*

"Fitzwilliam? Did you heed what I said, Fitzwilliam?"

Darcy came back to the present with a start. He realised that his aunt was addressing him and wondered desperately what the right response was. He had no idea what she had been saying. Thankfully, his mother came to his rescue:

"Your aunt was just suggesting that you might like to read to your cousin this morning," said Lady Anne, smiling at her son.

Lady Catherine nodded. "I have purchased a new book of poetry which Anne should enjoy. Her health, unfortunately, prevents her from reading herself—much too much strain for her eyes—but I know you should like to read to her, Fitzwilliam."

"Oh… er… certainly, Aunt," said Darcy, though there was nothing he wanted to do *less*.

He glanced at his cousin again and felt a small stab of guilt. It was not as if he really disliked Anne—in truth, he felt a bit sorry for her: cooped up in this great mausoleum of a house, with his aunt dictating her every move and no other children for company, save for the occasional visits from himself or one of his other cousins. Nevertheless, he had no wish to spend an entire morning in Anne's dreary company.

No, what he *really* longed to do was to go outside and try out that sled! It had been a stroke of luck finding the old sled in the hut at the rear of the estate. Benson, the Rosings Park head gardener, had helped him pull it out from beneath the pile of broken furniture and discarded gardening equipment, and cleaned it off for him. It was waiting for him now in the front foyer, and he was itching to try it out, especially since the new snowfall they'd had yesterday.

Darcy leaned slightly to the right to look out of the windows on the other side of the salon. He could see the glittering white banks of fresh snow beckoning to him. How he longed to be outside, feeling the cold pinching his cheeks and the wind rushing against him as he sailed downhill on the sled!

He stifled a sigh. Instead, he was forced to remain here, listening half-heartedly as the grown-ups conversed and trying to sit with his hands on his knees, his face the picture of courteous interest, as his father had instructed him. He looked across at Georgiana, who was being held in his mother's arms, and almost wished that he could be a baby like her. No one expected anything of Georgiana for she was barely a year old and could hardly even stand upright.

"I am going to write some letters now," said Lady Catherine, standing up from her armchair beside the fire. "You will want to attend to your correspondence too, I am sure," she said to Lady Anne.

"I believe I may go and lie down for a period," said Lady Anne as she handed

Georgiana over to the nurse, who had been standing quietly at the side of the room. “I am feeling a trifle fatigued.”

Darcy glanced at his mother. She had been looking pale lately and seemed to often be fatigued, spending much time in her room. He knew that Mother had had a hard time when Georgiana was born, but Father had always reassured him that she would recover with rest. He watched now as his father helped his mother solicitously to her feet.

“Fitzwilliam, you may come with me and Anne to the library—you may read to her there while I write my letters,” said Lady Catherine, waving her hand imperiously.

Darcy rose slowly, then on an impulse, turned to his parents and said, “Mother—Father—may I go outside for a short while first? I should like to have a go on the sled.” He looked eagerly at his father. “Can I? Please, sir?”

Lady Catherine frowned and started to say something but Mr Darcy interrupted her. He smiled and nodded at his son.

“All right, Fitzwilliam. I know you have been champing at the bit to give that sled a try.” He glanced out of the windows. “It looks like we have had some good snow. It would certainly be an excellent opportunity to test the sled.”

"But—" Lady Catherine started to protest.

"It is advantageous for Fitzwilliam to get some air and exercise," said Mr Darcy quietly but firmly. "Not good for the boy to be cooped up indoors all the time."

Lady Catherine compressed her lips into a thin line but did not say anything more.

"Thank you, sir!" cried Darcy happily, turning to leave the room.

"Wait. Fitzwilliam—" called Lady Catherine.

Darcy stopped and turned back warily. He hoped that his aunt would not ask him to take Anne out sledding with him. Then he remembered the way his cousin was cosseted and protected—surely there would be no chance of Lady Catherine allowing her out in this cold!

"Have care where you take the sled, Fitzwilliam," said Lady Catherine. "Make sure you stay away from the north side of the grounds, particularly near the pond. The hill there is very steep and you could have a bad fall."

"I *have* been sledding before," said Darcy indignantly. "I am not afraid of steep slopes—"

"Benson has advised me that the area is most dangerous," said Lady Catherine, giving him a stern look. "You are not to go there, is that understood?"

"Yes, yes, all right," said Darcy impatiently. Then before his aunt could say anything else, he turned and rushed out of the room.

Darcy sat up in the snow and laughed as he brushed some off his face. He got to his feet and righted the sled, which had flipped over as it hit a hump at the bottom of the hill. Thus far, the old sled was turning out to be everything he had hoped for. Despite the faded wood and old metal runners, it glided easily across the snow and ice. The only thing was... well, maybe it was not quite as fast as he could wish.

Darcy looked back up at the slope he had just come down and frowned. If only he could find a bigger hill! He was sure that with greater height, the sled would gain more momentum and therefore faster speed. He turned and scanned the snowy landscape, looking for a hill worthy of tackling. The grounds of Rosings Park stretched out around him. Darcy realised that he had come farther from the house than he had thought—he could see it now, small in the distance, the plumes of smoke rising from the chimneys. He doubted that they could see him so far away and felt pleased. He did not like the thought of Lady Catherine watching and judging his every move from the windows. It was nice to think of being outside her influence.

He turned and looked to the other side of the park. The ground sloped downwards in that direction and in the distance he could see a faint line running across the landscape. A fence, he realised. That must be the border with the neighbouring estate. And just before it, he saw that the land dipped, dropping away from sight.

There must be a sort of shelf there, Darcy realised. Maybe where the land suddenly dropped sharply downwards. A steep slope! He grabbed the rope on his sled and began to walk towards the ledge with mounting excitement, pulling the sled behind him. The snow crunched beneath his boots and he felt a few flakes drift down and land on his face, melting almost instantly. The cold nipped at his cheeks but he was pleasantly warm from his recent exertions and did not really mind.

Darcy arrived at the spot to see that his guess had been right. The land curved over the edge and swept downwards in a steep slope which ended beside a small pond surrounded by fir trees. The sight of the pond reminded him suddenly of his aunt's warning: *"Make sure you stay away from the north side of the grounds, particularly near the pond."* Had Lady Catherine meant this pond? He looked around. Yes, he was on the north side of Rosings Park, but he could see nothing that looked dangerous here. The snow lay in thick folds across the landscape and, below him, it covered the slope in a smooth layer of white powder which was particularly inviting. Everything looked pristine and peaceful.

Darcy thought of his cousin. Richard was a few years older than him and always seemed so confident and daring—he had told Darcy that he wanted to become an officer when he grew up. When he had been at Rosings together with Darcy in the past, he was always leading the way into fun and mischief. *If Richard were here*, Darcy thought, *he would not be hesitating. No, Richard would laugh and say, "Old Benson the gardener is just fussing for nothing!"*

Darcy set his sled down on the edge of the slope with sudden decision. He might be three years younger but he could be just as brave as his cousin! Quickly, he sat down on the sled, tucking his feet into position, then took a deep breath and looked down the slope once more. At the bottom, the surface of the pond gleamed dully and he realised that it must be frozen over. Perhaps he might investigate it when he reached the bottom—see if it might be suitable for a spot of ice-skating!

Eagerly, Darcy pushed off, giving a shout of delight as the sled dipped forwards, then shot downhill. He felt that familiar thrilling lurch in his stomach. The wind rushed into his face as he gathered speed and the landscape around him became a white blur as he went faster and faster…

… And faster…

The blinding snow began to make him dizzy. Darcy stretched his legs out, pushing his heels into the snow to attempt to slow the sled. But the snow was so soft that there was no resistance. The sled continued gaining speed as it rushed towards the bottom of the hill.

Darcy felt uneasy. The sled felt like it was careening out of control. He thrust his legs out harder, trying to keep his balance and remain upright as he jammed his heels into the snow. In vain, he threw his weight backwards but that only seemed to tilt the sled and cause it to shoot sideways down the slope.

"Ahhh!" cried Darcy, as the sled skidded and turned, then gave a great jolt as it hit something hard just beneath the surface of the snow.

The sled flipped.

Darcy was thrown through the air. Everything was upside down and spinning, then he felt himself dropping and saw the row of fir trees rushing up to meet him.

CRACK!

He landed on something hard. The breath was knocked from him and he cried out in pain. There was a terrible cracking sound and the next moment, he felt himself dropping again—only this time it was not through air but into icy water.

READ MORE:
Amazon | Amazon UK

www.penelopeswan.com

Also by Rose Fairbanks

Sisters Bewitched
Love Lasts Longest
A Sense of Obligation
No Cause to Repine
Undone Business
Letters from the Heart
The Gentleman's Impertinent Daughter

Acknowledgments

To my author friends Elizabeth, Leenie, Rosie, and Zoe that always were willing to hold my hand, nothing can take your place in my heart.

Thank you to the countless other people of the JAFF community who have inspired and encouraged me.

Last but not least I could never have written, let alone published, without the love and support of my beloved husband and babies!

About the Author

Rose Fairbanks fell in love with Mr. Fitzwilliam Darcy thirteen years ago. Coincidentally, or perhaps not, she also met her real life Mr. Darcy thirteen years ago. They had their series of missteps, just like Elizabeth and Darcy, but are now teaching the admiring multitude what happiness in marriage really looks like and have been blessed with two children, a four year old son and a two year old daughter.

Previously rereading her favorite Austen novels several times a year, Rose discovered Jane Austen Fan Fiction due to pregnancy-induced insomnia. Several months later she began writing.

Rose has a degree in history and hopes to one day finish her MA in Modern Europe and will focus on the Regency Era in Great Britain. For now, she gets to satiate her love of research, Pride and Prejudice, reading and writing....and the only thing she has to sacrifice is sleep! She proudly admits to her Darcy obsession, addictions to reading, chocolate, and sweet tea, is always in the mood for a good debate and dearly loves to laugh.

You can connect with Rose on Facebook, Twitter, and her blog: http://rosefairbanks.com

To join her email list for information about new releases and any other news, you can sign up here: http://eepurl.com/bmJHjn

Made in the USA
Coppell, TX
26 November 2019